LOST AND FOUND

Holly pointed back towards the bus shelter.

'Look!' she said. 'That man dropped his wallet. It fell on to the roof of the bus shelter.'

Miranda looked around. 'He's gone,' she said.

Holly nodded. 'I tried to tell him. I called to him. But he rushed off the bus.'

'Maybe he didn't hear you,' said Peter.

'He looked back,' said Holly. 'I'm sure he heard me.' She turned a worried face to her two friends. 'I think he did it on purpose.'

'Did what on purpose?' said Miranda.

'Threw his wallet away,' said Holly.

Peter and Miranda looked at her.

'Why on earth would anybody do that?' said Peter.

Holly shook her head and frowned. 'That's just what I'm wondering.'

The Mystery Kids series

THE MYSTERY KIDS
Lost and Found

Fiona Kelly

Hodder
Children's
Books

a division of Hodder Headline plc

Special thanks to Helen Magee

Copyright © 1995 Ben M. Baglio
Created by Ben M. Baglio
London W6 0HE

First published in Great Britain in 1995
by Hodder Children's Books

The right of Fiona Kelly to be identified as the Author of
the Work has been asserted by her in accordance with the
Copyright, Designs and Patents Act 1988.

10 9 8 7 6 5

All rights reserved. No part of this publication may be
reproduced, stored in a retrieval system, or transmitted,
in any form or by any means without the prior written
permission of the publisher, nor be otherwise circulated
in any form of binding or cover other than that in which
it is published and without a similar condition being
imposed on the subsequent purchaser.

All characters in this publication are fictitious and any
resemblance to real persons, living or dead, is purely
coincidental.

A Catalogue record for this book is
available from the British Library

ISBN 0 340 61990 2

Typeset by Hewer Text Composition Services, Edinburgh
Printed and bound in Great Britain by
Mackays of Chatham PLC, Chatham, Kent

Hodder Children's Books
A division of Hodder Headline plc
338 Euston Road
London NW1 3BH

Contents

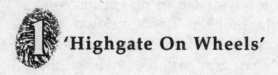# 1 'Highgate On Wheels'

'Holly!' Mrs Adams called from the front door. 'It's Miranda.'

As if Holly couldn't have guessed. Miranda Hunt's voice was one of the loudest Holly had ever heard. She could hear her right down the hall.

'Your mum's going shopping,' Miranda said, as she came into the sitting-room. 'She's taking Jamie with her.'

Holly grinned. Now they would get some peace. Jamie was Holly's little brother. He was nine, three years younger than Holly and a complete pest.

'She's getting him a new pair of school shoes,' Holly said. 'You can imagine how excited he was about *that*. Anyway, he's going because Mum promised him he could buy a Zappa Galactica with his birthday money.'

1

'A *what*?' said Miranda, pushing her long blonde hair back from her face.

Holly laughed. 'It's a space gun,' she said. 'He saw it advertised in one of his comics.'

Miranda plonked herself down on the sofa beside Holly and picked up a newspaper. 'That gun will be awfully noisy,' she said. 'And your brother is already a pain.'

Holly grinned. Miranda knew Jamie only too well.

'You know, we could write an article for this,' Miranda said, leafing through the newspaper.

Holly sat up, interested. She and Miranda edited *The Tom-tom*, the lower-school magazine at their school in North London.

'What about?' she said.

Miranda turned the pages of the newspaper. It was the free paper that everyone in Highgate got. It was mostly adverts and local news.

'I don't know,' said Miranda. 'Maybe if we could solve another mystery we could write it up.'

'Brilliant,' said Holly. 'The only trouble is, there aren't any mysteries to solve.'

2

'Rubbish!' said Miranda. 'The world is full of mysteries.'

'Too bad *Highgate* isn't,' said Holly.

But she was interested. Holly and Miranda and their friend Peter Hamilton had already solved a mystery – and got into the paper. The newspaper headline had called them the Mystery Kids. They had been famous – for a while. Why couldn't they do it again? All they needed was a mystery.

Holly began to think about spies and robbers. She was in the middle of a book about smugglers at the moment. Tonight, before she went to sleep, she would read the rest – and see if she had been right about the identity of the mastermind behind the smuggling operation.

Holly always tried to guess the solution to the mystery before she read the end of a book. She would write down clues as she went along and try to solve the mystery for herself. *Was it the housekeeper of the big old house on the cliffs?* she thought. *Or maybe it was the local doctor. He was a pretty suspicious character.*

She was miles away when Miranda spoke.

'There's a whole column about the parade

3

in here,' she said, looking at the newspaper. 'It looks terrific. Vintage buses and cars and stuff.'

'Let me see,' said Holly.

They were going to a parade in Highgate that afternoon, to mark the opening of a new transport museum. Holly looked over Miranda's shoulder. There was a big head-line saying 'Highgate On Wheels', spread across the top of the page.

'No wonder Peter wanted to go,' Miranda said.

Peter was mad about cars. He collected car registration numbers and fed them into his dad's computer. Holly and Miranda weren't sure why. But Peter was a boy, and they presumed boys did strange things like that.

Holly nodded. 'He'll get some really good registration numbers – old ones,' she said. 'There will be loads of old cars.'

Miranda grinned. 'Hey, I've got a joke: Why did the man drive his car into the lake?'

Holly screwed up her face. 'Tell me! Quick!' she said. 'Let's get it over with.'

'Because he wanted to dip the headlights,' said Miranda.

Holly rolled around the floor in mock pain. 'Miranda, that was terrible!'

Miranda giggled. 'I like it,' she said.

Miranda wrote a bad-jokes column for The *Tom-tom* – and she actually laughed at the jokes. And the worse the jokes were the more – and the louder – she laughed.

Holly looked at her friend. Miranda's head was buried in the newspaper again, scanning the small ads.

'What are you looking for?' she said.

Miranda looked up. 'I always read the small ads,' she said. 'It's amazing what you find in them.' She held up the paper. 'Look at this.'

Holly looked. The ad was in the 'Lost and Found' column. '"Lost in Highgate area – sewing machine in brown case. Reward offered",' she read out loud.

'How do you lose a sewing machine?' Miranda asked.

'Promise me this isn't another joke,' said Holly.

Miranda hooted with laughter. 'No, I'll let you off this time,' she said. She narrowed her eyes. 'But maybe we could find it and claim the reward.'

Holly frowned. 'Maybe it isn't really a sewing machine,' she said.

'Maybe it's a secret weapon disguised as a sewing machine!' said Miranda.

'And a foreign power is going to attack the Houses of Parliament with it!' said Holly.

'And we can find it and be national heroes,' said Miranda.

Holly and Miranda grinned at each other.

'Some chance,' they both said together.

'Come on,' said Holly. 'We promised we'd meet Peter at the shopping centre.'

Miranda looked up.

'What are these?' she said.

'What?' Holly said.

Miranda held out the paper. 'All these scribbles,' she said.

Holly drew herself up. 'Scribbles?' she said. 'Those are clues.'

Miranda looked at her. 'Clues for what?'

'I was watching this old mystery film on TV the other night,' Holly said. 'It was terrific.'

Miranda grinned. 'Did you solve it?' she said.

Holly bit her lip. 'Not exactly,' she said. 'In fact, not at all.'

Miranda was looking at Holly's notes all down the side of the newspaper. She shook her head. 'You'll never get anywhere just scribbling things down on bits of paper,' she said.

'I've run out of notebooks,' Holly said.

'Harriet the Spy never ran out of note-books,' said Miranda.

If Holly and Miranda had one favourite book in the world it was probably *Harriet the Spy* by Louise Fitzhugh. Holly's bed-room shelves were stacked with mystery books but it was *Harriet the Spy* that had really made her and Miranda want to be detectives.

'So, what was this mystery film about?' said Miranda.

Holly smiled. 'It was called *Charade*,' she said. 'It was about a search for a missing fortune.' She paused and frowned. 'But at the beginning, nobody knew what they were looking for.'

'So how do you find something when you don't know what you're looking for?' Miranda said.

Holly grinned. 'That was the whole point,' she said. 'It wasn't until the very end that they discovered the valuable thing they were looking for was a stamp.'

'So where did they find it?' said Miranda.

Holly's grin grew even wider. 'You'd never believe it,' she said.

Miranda's eyes lit up. 'Give me a clue and let me guess,' she said.

Holly looked at her watch. 'We don't have time if we're going to go to this parade.'

'OK,' said Miranda. 'Let's get going. You can tell me on the way. I bet it's really easy,' she said.

Holly laughed. 'We'll see,' she said. 'I know you'll never get it.'

'Bet I do,' said Miranda, opening the sitting-room door. Holly caught it before it crashed back into the standard lamp. Miranda was accident-prone.

'Never in a million years,' said Holly.

'What if I *do* guess?' Miranda said.

Holly considered. 'I'll let you read *The Clue of the Broken Angel* first,' she said. 'I haven't started it yet.'

Miranda's face lit up. *The Clue of the Broken*

8

Angel was the latest book by another of their favourite authors, and Holly had managed to get the last copy in the shop.

'Done!' said Miranda.

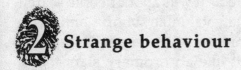 **Strange behaviour**

'So they found the stamp on an old envelope,' Holly finished, her face glowing. She and Miranda were waiting for Peter outside the shopping centre.

'What?' said Miranda. 'A stamp worth a fortune! Just stuck on an ordinary old envelope?'

Holly swept her long brown hair back from her forehead. The wind coming round the corner blew it back again. 'Yes,' she said. 'It was the perfect hiding-place. Who's going to look for a really valuable stamp on an envelope? You expect to see stamps on envelopes, so you don't take any notice of them. I told you you would never guess.'

Miranda looked up. 'There's Peter,' she said and started waving. 'Hey, Peter! Holly's telling me about this old film she saw on TV.'

11

'It was terrific,' said Holly. 'It was called *Charade*.'

'What was it about?' Peter said.

Holly laughed. 'It was about people searching for this really valuable stamp – and all the time it was hidden on a perfectly ordinary envelope. Just like an ordinary stamp.'

'That's a good trick,' Peter said admiringly.

Peter loved mysteries too – the stranger they were, the better. The best ones were real-life mysteries. But books and films were nearly as good.

Holly looked at her watch. 'Come on,' she said. 'I'll tell you more about the film as we go. We'll miss the parade if we don't hurry up!'

Soon, Holly, Peter and Miranda arrived at the parade. They could see the old cars and buses all lined up, waiting for the parade to begin.

'Look!' said Peter. 'There's an old open-topped bus.'

Holly and Miranda looked. The bus was a double-decker and the upper deck had no roof – just a guard-rail going round it.

'Oh,' said Holly. 'I'd love to have a ride on that!'

'So would I,' said Miranda. 'I've never been on an open-topped bus before.'

'Just think how much you could see from up there,' said Holly. 'You could do some terrific spying! I wish we could go on it.'

'Well, there's a man selling tickets,' said Peter, pointing.

A man in a peaked cap and an old-fashioned uniform was standing beside the bus. He had a shiny metal ticket machine on a leather strap slung over one shoulder and a leather bag over the other.

'Let's go for a ride,' suggested Peter.

Miranda looked doubtful. 'I don't know if you're allowed,' she said. 'All the people are going inside.'

'No, they aren't,' said Holly. 'Look! There's a man on the top deck.'

Peter grinned. 'What are we waiting for, then?' he said enthusiastically. He made a dash for the bus, leaving Miranda and Holly to catch up.

The three of them jumped on to the open platform at the back. The bus-conductor pushed down a lever on his ticket machine and out popped the tickets. He put their money in his bag.

'Can we go upstairs?' Miranda said eagerly.

The conductor smiled. 'Of course you can,' he said. 'You'll get a great view of the parade from up there. Just be careful you don't get blown away.'

'We won't,' said Miranda, making a dive for the twisting metal staircase. Holly and Peter were close behind her.

'Just in time!' said Holly as the bus started to move off.

'Wow!' Holly said as they came out on the top deck. 'Look at this. It's terrific.'

A gust of wind caught her hair and whipped it across her face. 'But windy,' she said. 'No wonder there isn't anybody on top.'

'Except that man,' said Miranda.

Holly looked. The man was sitting huddled up at the front of the bus. His hat was pulled down so it was almost over his ears.

'He doesn't look very happy,' said Holly. 'I wonder why he's up here and not downstairs.'

'He probably wants to see the parade better – like us,' said Miranda.

14

Holly cast another glance at the man in the hat. 'He isn't paying any attention to the parade,' she said.

'Who cares?' said Peter. 'We're off!'

The bus gave a lurch and the whole parade started moving. Holly, Peter and Miranda clung on to the guard-rail and hung over the side, watching the snaking line of cars and buses.

'Look! There's an old Rolls-Royce,' said Peter. 'And a Bentley – and a vintage Citroën.' He poked his head out further. 'Wow!' he yelled. 'A Model T Ford. This is amazing.'

Holly and Miranda looked at each other and grinned. Peter was already searching for his notebook to note down registration numbers.

Holly looked at the crowds swarming on the pavement.

'I feel rather important up here,' said Miranda. 'Do you think I should wave to the crowds?'

Holly looked down. The pavements were lined with people watching the parade go by. 'You mean, like the Queen?' she said.

Miranda laughed. Even out in the open, her voice was as loud as a foghorn. 'Yeah,'

15

she said. 'I should have brought my tiara.'
And she laughed again.

Peter covered his ears.

'Somebody should record your laugh,
Miranda,' he said.

Miranda looked at him. 'Why?' she said
suspiciously.

'They could use it as a fire alarm,' Peter
said. He ducked as Miranda made a dive
for him.

The man at the front of the bus looked
round and Holly caught a good view of his
face. He still didn't seem very happy. He
got up and went over to the other side of
the bus.

The bus lurched again.

'We're stopping,' said Peter.

The bus drew up at a bus shelter and a
line of old cars chugged past. Peter hung
over the rail, noting down numbers.

Miranda gave a squeal. 'Oh, look,' she
said. 'Over on the other side. Look at all the
old prams!' And she shot across and hung
over the other rail. A line of girls dressed
as old-fashioned nannies were wheeling
funny old prams along the pavement. 'Look,
Holly!' she said.

Holly moved to stand beside her. Then she grinned.

'"Highgate On Wheels,"' she said. 'I suppose that includes prams.'

Miranda laughed. 'Look at the size of them! You could get ten babies in each one.'

The bus lurched again as it started to move away from the bus shelter. Holly staggered slightly. Out of the corner of her eye she saw the man with the hat stand up and lean over the rail. Holly clutched the rail to steady herself.

'Look at this!' Peter yelled from the other side of the bus.

Miranda turned but Holly's eyes were on the man with the hat. He was leaning right over the rail. His back was towards her. He seemed to be looking at someone in the crowd.

A policeman was trying to clear a path through the crowds on the pavement for the nannies and their prams. Holly saw him move a group of onlookers aside. Some of them didn't want to move. One man was moving very slowly indeed. He looked up and his eyes met Holly's. Then the policeman spoke to him and he moved slowly away.

Holly turned to the man on the bus. He was looking at the policeman and there was a funny expression on his face. Holly stared at him. He had small dark eyes and a pointed face. She thought he looked just like a ferret.

She saw him put his hand in his pocket and take something out of it. He fumbled for a moment, then his arm jerked. Something dropped over the rail and on to the roof of the bus shelter. Holly stared at the object lying on top of the bus-shelter roof. It seemed to be made of leather. Holly gasped. It was a wallet.

The man with the hat brushed past her, almost running down the centre passage of the bus. Holly turned. 'Hey!' she called after him. 'You've dropped your wallet!'

The man had reached the top of the stairs. He turned and looked back at Holly. Then he dived down the stairs.

'Hey!' Holly called again.

But the man had gone. Holly hung over the rail and watched as he jumped off the platform of the moving bus and disappeared into the crowd.

'Who are you shouting at?' said Peter, coming over to stand beside her.

Holly pointed back towards the bus shelter.

'Look!' she said. 'That man dropped his wallet. It fell on to the roof of the bus shelter.'

Miranda looked round. 'He's gone,' she said.

Holly nodded. 'I know,' she said. 'I tried to tell him. I called to him. But he rushed off the bus.'

'Maybe he didn't hear you,' said Peter.

'Maybe not,' said Holly. 'But he looked back. I'm sure he heard me.'

'He probably thought you were yelling at us,' said Miranda.

Holly looked uncertain.

'What's wrong?' said Peter. 'We can go back and fetch the wallet.'

'That's right,' said Miranda. 'There's bound to be something in it with his address on it. We can post it to him or give it to a policeman or something. It's lucky you saw it happen. He'll get it back.'

Holly shook her head. 'It isn't *that* I'm bothered about,' she said.

'What is it then?' said Peter. He was looking at her closely. 'Something's up, Holly. What is it?'

Holly turned a worried face to her two friends. 'I can't be sure,' she said. 'But I think he did it on purpose.'

'Did what on purpose?' said Miranda.

'Threw his wallet away,' said Holly.

Peter and Miranda looked at her.

'Why on earth would anybody do that?' said Peter.

Holly shook her head and frowned. 'That's just what I'm wondering,' she said.

The blue ticket

'Let's go and get that wallet now,' Holly said.

'But we've only just got on the bus,' said Miranda. 'We'll miss all the fun.'

Holly turned to her. 'Look,' she said. 'This could be a real mystery. What if we miss *that*?'

Miranda didn't look convinced.

'Peter?' said Holly.

Peter ran a hand through his hair. 'Are you sure you aren't still thinking about that film?' he said to Holly.

Holly shook her head. 'I'm sure there's something funny going on,' she said. 'I'm telling you, that man threw his wallet away as soon as he saw the policeman.'

Peter's eyes lit up. 'Maybe it isn't *his* wallet,' he said. 'Maybe he's a pick-pocket. Look at the crowds. You always get pick-pockets

21

when there are big crowds like this.'

'But if he was a pick-pocket he would have stolen whatever was in the wallet,' Miranda said. 'Why throw it away otherwise? That means the wallet must be empty.'

'He might have taken just the money and credit cards. There might be a name and address in it,' said Holly. 'We could return it to its rightful owner.'

'Maybe even get a reward!' said Peter.

'And if we find the owner and that man really *is* a pick-pocket, we can give his description to the police,' said Holly.

Peter looked doubtful. 'I don't know if *I* could,' he said. 'He had a hat on. I wasn't taking any notice of him.'

But Holly stood her ground. 'I could describe him,' she said. 'He looked like a ferret.'

'You can't tell the police that,' said Miranda.

'So you think he *might* be a pick-pocket?' said Holly.

'No . . . But Miranda didn't sound so sure.'

'Come on,' Peter said to Miranda. 'It certainly looks suspicious.' He grinned. 'And they didn't call us the Mystery Kids for nothing,' he said. 'We could be on to something here.'

Peter and Holly looked at Miranda.

'Oh, all right,' she said. 'But I bet it's just a mouldy old wallet that he was finished with.'

'I'll bet it isn't,' said Holly. 'Let's go – the bus is nearly at the next stop.'

'I'm with you, Holly,' said Peter, as he made a dive for the stairs and swung himself out on the handrails. He looked over his shoulder at them. 'Come on, what are you waiting for?' he yelled. 'Go for it, Mystery Kids!' and he disappeared round the bend in the stairs.

Holly and Miranda followed. They hurtled past the surprised bus-conductor.

'Hey!' he shouted after them as they leaped off. 'I thought you wanted to ride in the parade.'

Holly waved. 'We'll catch you up,' she said.

The conductor scratched his head. 'I suppose you will,' he said. 'We aren't going anywhere fast, not with this crowd.' He leaned out, wrapping his arm round the pole of the platform. 'Remember to hold on to your tickets,' he said. 'I can't let you back on without a ticket.'

'We will,' Holly said. She began to run back where the bus had just come from.

Holly had a stitch in her side by the time she reached the bus shelter.

'I hope nobody else finds the wallet before we do,' said Holly to Peter.

Miranda caught up with them just in time to catch Holly's last words. 'Nobody else is even interested,' she said. 'You'll see – it'll just be a smelly old wallet.'

'Maybe,' said Holly, 'and maybe not.' She turned to Peter. 'Right then, you're the best climber.'

Peter looked at the bus shelter and sighed. 'Thanks a *lot*!' he said. He began to climb up the pole of the bus stop.

'Mind the roof doesn't collapse,' called Miranda, as Peter transferred his weight from the pole to the bus-shelter roof.

'Oh, thanks for the warning,' he called back. 'I really appreciate that.'

'Have you found it?' Holly yelled.

Peter's face appeared over the edge of the bus-shelter roof. 'Got it!' he said.

Peter tossed the wallet down to her.

Holly jumped up to catch it and landed on someone's toes.

'Sorry,' she said.

The woman gave her a severe look. Then she looked up at Peter on top of the bus shelter.

'Disgraceful,' she said. 'Hooligans!'

Holly watched the woman disappear into the jostling crowd.

'Well?' Miranda said in her ear. 'What's in it?'

Holly opened the wallet. Nothing!

'It's empty,' she said to Miranda.

Miranda shrugged. 'What did I tell you?' she said. 'It's just an old wallet. Look at it! It's all tatty.'

'Bad luck, Holly,' Peter called down.

'Come down, Peter,' Miranda called back.

Peter grinned. 'In a minute,' he said. 'I've got this great view of a 1958 Humber from up here. I think I can get the number.'

Holly looked at the wallet. It was coming to bits. The leather was split and the lining was torn.

'Wait a minute,' she said. 'There *is* something in it. Down here, behind the torn lining.'

'What?' said Miranda.

Holly fumbled in the lining and pulled

out a crumpled piece of blue paper. She smoothed it out. It was perforated down one edge – as if it had been torn off another bit of paper.

'There's a number on it. It looks like a ticket,' she said.

'A ticket!' said Miranda. 'Some mystery. Just a stupid old bus ticket.'

Holly peered at the ticket. 'It doesn't look like a bus ticket,' she said. 'Look!' She held it out for Miranda to see.

At that moment somebody barged straight into Holly, knocking her sideways. She almost dropped the ticket.

'Oops!' she said, as a man's hand caught her arm. 'Sorry!'

She looked up into the man's face. She had seen it somewhere before. *That's it! He was the man I saw in the crowd from the bus.*

'Hoi!' called a voice.

Holly whipped round. A policeman was making his way towards them.

'Hoi!' he called again. 'Get down off there.'

He was looking at Peter.

'Cripes!' said Peter. He dived off the bus-shelter roof, then slid down the pole.

They watched the policeman trying to decide whether to bother pushing his way through the crowd.

'Let's get out of here before that policeman gets to us,' said Peter.

Holly was staring after the man who had barged into her. He was walking quickly through the crowds. Then she lost sight of him.

'There's nothing in the wallet,' Miranda said to Peter. 'Except an old ticket.'

'We don't want that policeman getting the wrong idea,' Peter said, taking the wallet from Holly's hands. He tossed it back on to the bus-shelter roof. 'There!' he said.

'Why did you do that?' said Holly.

Peter frowned. 'We can't trace the owner,' he said. 'We might as well leave it where he dropped it in case he comes back for it.'

'And if he's a pick-pocket?' said Holly.

Peter shrugged. 'It's a tatty old wallet. There's no address in it and we've got no proof.'

Holly bit her lip.

'Cheer up,' said Peter. 'At least I got a couple of really good registration numbers from up there.'

Holly smiled in spite of herself. Peter looked really pleased with his car numbers.

'Come on!' said Miranda. 'The policeman is getting closer.'

Holly gave the ticket a last look and put it in her pocket.

They wriggled their way through the crowd.

'Let's try to catch up with the bus,' said Miranda.

As they made their way back to the bus, Holly went over and over in her mind the scene on the top of the bus. There *was* something mysterious about it. She just *knew* there was. Why had the man deliberately dropped his wallet? And what had he seen that had frightened him?

'You're back,' said the bus-conductor as they panted up to the next stop.

'And we've got our tickets!' Peter said.

Holly shoved her hand in her pocket and drew out the ticket she had found in the wallet.

'This isn't a bus ticket, is it?' she said to the conductor.

The conductor took it and looked at it.

'No,' he said, shaking his head. 'Looks

more like a left-luggage ticket or something to me.' He peered closer. 'There's a number but nothing to say what it's for.' He shrugged. 'Sorry.'

Peter looked at Holly as they emerged on to the top deck. 'You really *do* think there's something funny going on, don't you?' he said.

Holly nodded. 'I'm sure of it,' she said. 'What if you're right? What if he really *is* a pick-pocket? He shouldn't get away with it.'

Peter and Miranda looked at each other. Miranda shrugged.

'If you really want to investigate this, maybe we could trace the owner of the wallet through the ticket,' Peter said to Holly. 'We could find out if it has been stolen.'

'But there isn't anything on it,' Holly said. 'Only a number.'

'Let's see,' he said. Holly handed the ticket to him and he peered at it. 'Beats me,' he said, at last.

'The bus-conductor says it might be a left-luggage ticket,' Holly said.

Miranda looked at her. 'Maybe it's the pick-pocket's ticket, after all,' she said. 'Maybe if

29

we trace it, we'll find a suitcase full of stolen money or something. You know, where he's stashed all his loot.'

Holly's eyes lit up. 'We might,' she said.

Miranda shook her head. 'You never give up, do you?' she said. 'I was only joking.'

Holly grinned. 'But *I'm not* joking,' she said. 'This *is* a mystery. After all, I was the one who saw the Ferret throw the wallet away.'

'Who?' said Miranda.

'The Ferret,' said Holly. 'That's what he looked like – a ferret. I tell you, there was something funny about him.'

'There *would* be if he looked like a ferret!' said Miranda.

'OK, OK,' said Peter. 'So, what do we do now then?'

Holly thought. 'First things first,' she said. 'We write everything down.'

Peter grinned. 'We can call it *The Ferret File*,' he said.

Holly grinned back at him. They were on the trail. *The Mystery Kids ride again*, she thought.

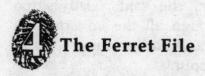

4 The Ferret File

'What are you looking for?' Miranda said to Holly.

The Mystery Kids were on their way home from the parade.

'I need to buy a notebook,' Holly said.

'And I need to buy a newspaper, so I can look at the houses for sale,' Peter said.

'Are you still looking for a house?' Holly said.

Peter nodded. 'The flat really is too small for us. Dad needs a room he can use as an office.'

Peter and his father lived on their own. Peter's mum had died when he was little. They had moved into a flat not far from Holly's house when they first came to Highgate, but it had always been a temporary arrangement.

'Don't move too far away,' Miranda said.

31

'We don't want to split the Mystery Kids up.'

Peter grinned. 'Why do you think I'm buying the paper?' he said. 'Dad is too busy to look through all the adverts so I go through them and choose some for him to have a think about.'

'Let me guess,' said Miranda. 'All the ones you "select" are nearby.'

'Right first time,' said Peter. 'Though I do pick ones in other areas which are too big or too expensive or— '

'We get the picture,' said Miranda. 'Peter Hamilton, you're a disgrace. Your dad's a very trusting guy!'

'Here's a newsagent,' said Holly. 'We'll get a notebook there.'

'I really wish we could find a house soon,' Peter said. 'I'm getting fed up with the flat. And I'd like a garden.'

They went into the shop. Peter bought an *Evening Standard* and Holly searched the shelves for a notebook. Miranda headed straight for a shelf of paperback mysteries.

Holly took a notebook from a display shelf. She wrinkled her nose as she looked at it. But there wasn't much to choose from, so it would have to do. She paid the woman at the counter, then hauled Miranda away from a paperback with a knife dripping blood on the cover.

'You'll give yourself nightmares,' she said.

Miranda rolled her eyes dramatically. 'It was called *The Curse of the Doomed*,' she said.

Peter looked up from his paper and twisted his face up into a horrible shape. Miranda giggled and Holly shoved them both out on to the pavement.

'Now we can start making notes,' she said.

Miranda looked at the notebook in disgust. 'In *that*?' she said. 'You must be joking.'

'What's wrong with it?' Holly said innocently. But she knew what was the matter with it.

Peter was staring at it as if he couldn't believe his eyes. 'It's got fluffy bunnies all over it,' he said.

'It was the best they had,' Holly said. 'It was either bunnies or kittens!'

'How can you expect us to take this investigation of yours seriously if we've got to write things down in a fluffy bunny notebook?' said Peter.

'Harriet the Spy's notebook didn't have fluffy bunnies on it,' said Miranda.

'It doesn't matter what it's got *on* it,' said Holly. 'It's what we put *in* it that matters.'

'That'll give me more nightmares than *The Curse of the Doomed*,' said Miranda.

'Just don't expect me to be seen with it,' Peter said.

'Or me,' said Miranda.

Holly sighed. Sometimes it was really difficult to keep to the point with these two.

'I'm starving,' said Miranda. 'I can't think on an empty stomach.'

'Nor can I,' said Peter.

'So let's go and get something to eat,' said Holly. 'Then we can make a start on the investigation.'

But all the fast food places in Highgate were full to bursting-point.

'All the other people who were at the parade must have had the same idea,' said Peter.

'We could go to my house,' said Miranda.

Peter and Holly groaned.

'Not if Rachel and Becky are there,' said Holly.

Rachel and Becky were Miranda's twin sisters. They were fifteen and they thought they were really grown-up.

'We never get any peace when they're around,' said Peter. 'How about the flat?' Then his face fell. 'Dad's working at home today,' he said.

Holly grinned. 'If you promise not to make any more comments about the bunny notebook, we can go to my house,' she said. 'Mum went shopping today so the fridge will be full – if Jamie hasn't eaten everything already.'

'Comments?' said Peter. 'Who's making comments? We love the notebook! Let's go.'

'It was only a bit of artistic criticism,' Miranda said loftily. '*I* think you should have gone for the kittens.'

They were still arguing when they got back to Holly's house.

'What's that noise?' Miranda asked as they reached the front door. A peculiar sound was coming from inside the house.

Holly opened the door and Jamie rushed

past them. He had a lethal-looking black gun in his hands.

'Look what I've got!' he yelled at them. He pointed the gun at them and a strobing light flashed. A high-pitched whining noise rose to deafening pitch and the gun began to give out an amazingly loud clatter. The noise was awful.

'Wow!' said Peter. 'It's a Zappa Galactica. I wouldn't mind one of those.'

'You're too old for toy guns,' Miranda said.

Peter drew himself up. 'Toy gun!' he said, outraged. 'That isn't a toy gun. It's a state-of-the-art, fully automated replica.'

'Oh, yeah!' said Miranda. 'It still looks like a toy gun to me.'

'Girls!' Peter said to Jamie, shaking his head.

Jamie gave Miranda an extra blast with the gun, backing his way down the garden path. Holly put her hands over her ears as she watched her brother dash out of the front gate, still zapping everything in sight.

'Make yourselves a snack,' said Mrs Adams as they came in.

Peter and Miranda made a dive for the kitchen. They never had to be asked twice to eat.

Holly looked at her mum. 'How on earth did he manage to get you to buy him that?' she said.

Mrs Adams shook her head. 'Don't ask,' she said. 'It was a moment of weakness. And it *was* his birthday money. And, to cap it all, he didn't get any shoes. I ended up taking his old ones to the menders.' She smiled. 'For some reason he likes those old shoes. And now he's gone to show Martin his Zappa Galactica, I can put my feet up for half an hour.'

Holly grinned. 'We won't disturb you,' she said. 'We're going to have a conference in the kitchen.'

'It's just as well I did some shopping then,' Mrs Adams said as she went into the sitting-room.

'Tuna or peanut butter on your sandwich, Holly?' Miranda's voice boomed from the kitchen.

Holly hurried down the hall. If her mum wanted peace and quiet she needed a couple of closed doors between her and Miranda.

37

'Tuna,' she said, coming into the kitchen and sitting down at the table. She took out the new notebook.

Peter plonked three glasses of milk and a plate of sandwiches down on the table and sat down beside her.

'Oh, thanks,' said Holly.

She was already writing, heading the first page *THE FERRET FILE*.

She underlined it. Then she wrote down three questions:

1. *Why did the Ferret throw the wallet away?*
2. *What made him look so shifty?*
3. *What is the ticket for?*

Peter shook his head. 'I can't believe you're actually using that notebook,' he said. He looked closely at it. 'Look, it's got bunnies on every page!'

'It'll do until we can get a better one,' she said, frowning as she tried to think.

'Like this mystery of yours,' said Miranda. 'That'll do until we get a better one too, I suppose.'

Holly put both elbows on the table and leaned forward, looking at Peter and Miranda.

'Now,' she said in her most serious voice. 'What about answers to these questions?'

'OK,' said Peter, 'fire away.'

Holly cleared her throat and read from her notebook.

'"Why did the Ferret throw the wallet away?"'

'Because he had stolen all the money out of it and he wanted to get rid of the evidence,' Peter said. He took a bite of his sandwich.

Holly wrote down *Pick-pocket – getting rid of evidence*.

'Any more ideas?' she said.

'Because it was just an old wallet and he'd bought a new one,' Miranda said.

Holly wrote down *No mystery, just an old wallet*.

'What about the next question?' she said. 'Why was he looking so shifty?'

Peter and Miranda both shrugged.

'We didn't see him,' Peter said. 'You were the only one who saw him.'

'I *know* that,' said Holly. 'But why do you think he was looking the way he was looking?'

'It could have been because he was afraid

he would get into trouble for dropping litter,'
Miranda said.

Holly shook her head. 'He didn't look the
type to worry about that,' she said, but she
wrote it down anyway.

'If he *was* a pick-pocket, he would be
watching out to see if anybody was watching
him,' said Peter.

'Good thinking,' Holly said, and she wrote
that down too.

She thought for a moment. 'I'm sure he
was keeping an eye on that policeman,' she
said. 'He didn't throw the wallet away until
the policeman had turned his back.'

'OK,' said Peter. 'Put down that he had
something to hide from the police. That
covers a lot of ground.'

'Right,' said Holly, sitting up straight. 'If
we're going to solve this mystery we have
to find out who the wallet belongs to.
So really the third question is the most
important.' She looked at Peter and Miranda,
making sure she had their full attention.
'What I want us to do,' she said, 'is to
think of all the things you can get tickets for.'

'The zoo,' said Miranda. Then she got that

look in her eyes. 'Peter, what's a crocodile's favourite game?'

'Snap!' he said.

'Spoilsport,' said Miranda.

'I'm serious,' Holly said.

'OK,' said Peter. He thought for a moment. 'There are bus tickets and cinema tickets.'

'And parking-tickets and train tickets,' Miranda joined in.

'And raffle-tickets and concert tickets,' Peter added.

'And plane tickets and cloakroom tickets,' Miranda sang back.

Holly looked up. 'Are you two taking this seriously?' she said.

'Of course we are,' said Peter.

'You've got to admit it,' said Miranda. 'You can get tickets for nearly everything.'

Holly frowned. When you thought about it, Miranda was right.

'At least we can cross some off the list,' she said. 'I mean it isn't a plane ticket, is it?'

Peter and Miranda looked at the scrap of blue paper.

'No, I suppose not,' said Peter. Then he looked up. 'It's perforated,' he said. 'Look, you can see where it's been torn off another piece of paper.'

'The other half of the ticket,' Holly said. 'It's like one of those mysteries where you get half a coin and you have to find the other half, the bit that fits.'

'John Raven had to solve a mystery like that,' said Miranda. 'Do you remember the episode?'

Secret Agent John Raven was the star of *Spyglass*, the Mystery Kids' favourite TV programme.

'That was the one where he had half the piece of paper with the secret code on it and he had to find the other half,' said Peter.

'John Raven found a defect in the paper and matched it up that way,' said Miranda.

'We can't do that,' said Peter. 'I mean it's a perfectly ordinary perforation. There must be loads more of those tickets with perforations just like that.'

'And we'd still have to find out what kind of ticket it is first,' said Holly.

Suddenly the task seemed impossible.

Peter must have seen the disappointment in her face.

'But it's got a number on it,' he said.

'769432. That should help. If we can work out what kind of ticket it is, then we should be able to match it up.'

'*If* the other half of the ticket has a number on it as well,' said Miranda.

'What kinds of tickets have numbers on both parts?' said Holly.

They all sat there munching their sandwiches and drinking milk. Then Peter said, 'Raffle-tickets. They have to have numbers on both bits so that you know who's won.'

Miranda sat up, interested at last.

'A winning raffle-ticket!' she said. 'Maybe we could claim the prize.' She laughed. 'With our luck it would probably be a fluffy bunny!'

Holly poked her tongue out at her.

'It could be a lottery ticket,' said Peter.

Holly frowned. 'Wouldn't there be more information on it?' she said.

Peter shrugged. 'If only there was something else on it – *anything* else. It would give us a clue. But a number! It could be anything.'

'The bus-conductor said it looked like a left-luggage ticket,' said Holly.

'Or it could be for a storage company,' said

Peter. 'You know – people put things into storage if they're going abroad for a while.'

Miranda looked doubtful. 'It doesn't look important enough for that,' she said. 'I mean if you're storing furniture or stuff, wouldn't you get a list with all the things on it?'

'*I* still think it might be a left-luggage ticket,' Holly said.

'Even if it is,' said Miranda, 'how do we find out where the left-luggage office is?'

'What kind of places have left-luggage offices?' said Peter.

Holly thought for a moment. 'Railway stations,' she said. 'All big stations have left-luggage offices – don't they?'

Peter shook his head. 'Search me,' he said. Then he brightened. 'But we can go and look.'

'When?' said Holly.

'Where?' said Miranda.

'Euston,' Peter said. 'Tomorrow. We can take the tube straight there.'

'Or St Pancras or King's Cross,' said Holly.

'OK,' said Peter. 'If we have no luck at Euston, we'll try the other London stations.' He opened his newspaper.

'What if we have no luck at any of them?' said Miranda.

'Then we'll just have to think again,' said Holly. 'In the meantime, keep thinking about things you get tickets for – just in case it isn't a left-luggage ticket.'

'OK,' said Miranda.

The two girls looked at Peter. He had his head buried in the *Evening Standard*.

'Peter!' said Miranda.

He didn't look up.

'Peter!' Holly said loudly. 'Those houses can't be *that* interesting.'

Peter looked up. 'What?' he said. 'No, that wasn't what I was reading. Look at this. There's been a robbery in Highgate!'

'What kind of robbery?' said Holly.

'From a jewellery exhibition,' Peter said. 'The paper says the thief got away with a brooch worth thousands of pounds. He left a dummy brooch in the display case and they didn't discover the switch until they were closing up at night and found the alarms had been cut.'

Holly sighed. 'I wish we had a mystery like *that* to solve instead of trying to find out about tickets!'

Peter grinned at her. 'Fat chance,' he said.

Miranda's face took on a dreamy look. 'Stolen jewels worth thousands of pounds,' she said. Then her mouth turned down. 'And all we get to investigate is a stupid ticket!'

 On the trail

By next morning Holly was beginning to wonder if Miranda was right. Maybe they didn't have a real mystery to investigate. But she was still thinking about the ticket during breakfast.

'Holly, are you going to eat anything this morning?' Mrs Adams asked.

Holly looked up. 'Oh, sorry, Mum,' she said. 'I was thinking.'

'What about?' said Jamie.

'Tickets,' Holly said.

Jamie's face lit up. 'Dad,' he said. 'Martin has an extra ticket for the football match on Saturday. Can I go?'

Mr Adams looked up. 'Don't talk to me about tickets,' he said. 'I got a whopper of a parking-ticket yesterday and I was only five minutes over time on the meter.'

Holly shook her head. 'Not that kind of

ticket,' she said. 'Maybe like a left-luggage ticket.' Jamie started badgering Mr Adams about the football match and Holly gave up trying to get a word in. Then an idea occurred to her. She turned to her mum.

'Mum, you know you have safe-deposit boxes at the bank . . .'

Mrs Adams was assistant bank manager in a local bank. She nodded.

'How do they work?' Holly said. 'Do you give the person a ticket?'

Mrs Adams shook her head. 'No,' she said. 'We give them a key. Some of the really big banks have computerised codes.'

'No tickets?' said Holly.

'No tickets,' her mum said with a smile. 'This wouldn't happen to be another mystery by any chance?'

Holly grinned. 'Sort of,' she said.

Mr Adams shook his head. 'Holly, you see a mystery round every corner.'

'The only mystery *I'm* interested in is whether or not you're going to eat your breakfast,' said Mrs Adams.

'Sorry,' Holly said. She started eating.

But the question bothered her. What *was* that ticket for? She was still thinking about it when she set out to meet Peter and Miranda.

Today, Holly told herself. *We'll start the real investigation today*.

By the time she saw Peter and Miranda waiting outside Highgate tube station she was feeling quite cheerful again.

'We'll try Euston,' said Peter. 'It's on our branch of the Northern Line.'

'OK,' said Holly. 'And if they don't have a left-luggage office there we can try King's Cross and St Pancras which are nearby.'

They got their tickets from the machine and made their way along the crowded platform.

'I've got a huge list of things you can get tickets for,' Holly said as the train came in.

'Let's see,' said Miranda.

Holly opened her notebook as the crowd jostled towards the doors of the train.

Somebody bumped her. 'Ouch!' she said, looking round and rubbing her elbow. A man was getting into the train the next door along. He looked a little familiar.

'Come on,' Peter shouted. Holly looked up and made a dash for the train just as the doors started closing.

Miranda was waving furiously at her.

'Come on!' she yelled. She wedged herself in the doorway, holding back the doors with her hands and feet.

Holly dived under Miranda's outstretched arm and the doors sprang open again.

'Hey! You kids! Get away from the doors!' shouted a guard on the platform.

Miranda poked her head out of the door. 'I was just saving my friend from a horrible death,' she called to the guard. 'She might have got crushed in the doors.'

The guard started to walk towards them as the train doors began to shut again.

Peter hauled Miranda inside. The doors closed and the train drew out of the station.

'Going by the look on that guy's face, it was *you* that just escaped a horrible death,' Holly said to Miranda.

Miranda looked offended. 'And that's all the thanks you get for saving a person's life.'

Holly laughed. 'Thanks,' she said. 'Will that do?'

'I suppose,' said Miranda.

'What were you doing anyway?' Peter said to Holly.

Holly shrugged. 'I thought I recognised that man.'

'Which man?' Miranda said.

Holly looked round. She couldn't see him anywhere. 'I think he went into the next carriage,' she said. 'He bumped into me.'

'No wonder, in this crowd,' said Peter. 'Let's see the notes you made, Holly.'

Holly gave him her notebook as the three of them wedged themselves into two seats.

'You're right about it being a long list,' said Peter.

Holly bit her lip. 'I just kept thinking of more and more things you can get tickets for. It's amazing.'

'I don't think we'll ever find out what that ticket is for,' said Miranda. 'There are just too many possibilities.'

'Well, it isn't for a safe-deposit box,' Holly said. 'I asked Mum about that.'

'And it isn't for a storage company,' Peter said. 'I phoned a few when I got home yesterday and they said everything was computerised these days.'

'Let's go through the list,' said Miranda. 'We're bound to come up with something.'

But by the time they got to Euston they

51

were nowhere nearer to solving the puzzle. Miranda had started a list of her own.

'Madame Tussaud's,' she said as the train drew into Euston. 'Maybe somebody has hidden a body in the Chamber of Horrors.'

'Maybe it's a ticket for the Tower of London and a plan to steal the Crown Jewels,' said Peter. He looked at Miranda, who seemed to be considering the possibility. 'It's a joke,' he said.

They tumbled out of the carriage. Holly looked round, trying to spot the man who had shoved past her.

'Come on, Holly!' Peter shouted.

Holly followed Peter and Miranda through the crowds and into the railway station. But she kept looking back. *Was someone watching them?*

Peter was talking to a man in a railway uniform when she caught up with them.

'Show him the ticket,' Miranda whispered.

Holly put her hand in her pocket to get the ticket but Peter shook his head.

'Don't bother,' he said.

'Why?' said Miranda.

'Because the guard says all the left luggage

goes in lockers – with keys. And it's the same at King's Cross and St Pancras.'

'There *are* other stations,' Holly said.

Peter looked disappointed. 'He says they're all the same.'

'So we're back where we started,' said Miranda. 'I knew it – it's just a boring old unimportant ticket. It's probably for a sports centre or some laundry or something.'

Peter nodded. 'You know, Miranda is probably right,' he said. 'What's so mysterious about a ticket stuck in the lining of an old wallet?'

Holly's heart sank. But she couldn't forget the look on the Ferret's face as he threw the wallet away. Suspicious – that's what it was. He wasn't just tossing away an old wallet. There was more to it than that. They couldn't just give up now.

'Maybe we aren't looking at it quite right,' Holly said.

'How do you mean?' said Peter.

Holly frowned. 'I don't know,' she said. She thought for a moment. 'Maybe it's like that film.'

'*Charade*?' said Miranda.

Holly nodded. 'Yes,' she said. 'Maybe it's

just a question of seeing something we've missed – something that's staring us in the face. I mean, in the film they couldn't see the answer for looking at it. The envelope was there all the time – with the stamp on it.'

'But the ticket doesn't tell us anything,' said Peter.

'No,' Holly said slowly. 'It doesn't, does it?'

'So what can we do?' said Miranda.

But Holly wasn't listening. She turned a shining face to the other two. 'Maybe Miranda *is* right,' she said.

'What?' said Miranda, as if she couldn't believe her ears.

'Maybe the ticket isn't important,' she said.

'You mean you're going to give up on the mystery?' said Peter.

Holly's eyes were alight. 'No way!' she said. 'Only, maybe it isn't the ticket that's important. Maybe it's the wallet that's important.'

'But it was empty,' said Peter.

Holly nodded. 'Exactly,' she said. 'The ticket was stuck down behind the lining. The Ferret probably didn't even know it was there. But he still threw the wallet away when he saw the policeman.'

'So?' said Miranda.

'So maybe we should go back and take another look at that wallet,' said Holly.

Peter gave a whoop. 'Holly, you might be on to something there. Come on, what are we waiting for?' He headed off towards the entrance to the Underground station.

Holly and Miranda started after him. Holly glanced round quickly.

'What are you looking at?' said Miranda.

Holly opened her mouth to tell her she felt somebody was watching them, then she decided not to. After the business with the ticket, she was certain Miranda would only laugh.

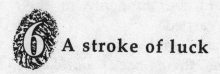 **A stroke of luck**

'Well, *that* was a wasted journey,' said Miranda as they got off the train at Highgate.

'No, it wasn't,' Holly said. 'Now we know it must be the wallet that's important.'

'So let's go and get it,' said Peter.

'Now?' said Holly.

Peter shrugged. 'Why not?'

'OK,' said Miranda. 'But I still don't think there's any mystery.'

They rounded the corner into the High Street. Holly and Miranda were still arguing. Suddenly Peter stopped in his tracks. Holly and Miranda bumped into him.

'What's wrong?' said Holly.

Peter was looking at the bus shelter. 'There's a workman at the shelter,' he said.

Holly looked. Sure enough, a man in blue overalls was putting a short ladder up against the bus shelter. Holly frowned as she watched him climb on to the bus shelter roof.

'He'll find the wallet,' Miranda said.

As the man turned suddenly in their direction, Holly gasped.

'Get back!' she said quietly to the others, dragging them back round the corner.

'What did you do that for?' Peter said.

'Don't you recognise him?' Holly said. 'It's the Ferret!'

'The man who threw the wallet away?' asked Miranda.

Holly nodded. 'And what do you think he's doing up there?' she said. 'Why do you think he's wearing overalls?'

'Looking for the wallet,' said Peter. 'You were right.'

'Maybe he's just doing his job,' said Miranda. 'Maybe he's just fixing the bus shelter.'

'There's nothing wrong with the bus shelter,' Holly said. 'He's wearing overalls so that people will *think* he's some kind of workman. People don't just climb up on to bus-shelter roofs – not unless they're up to something. He's trying to pretend he's got a right to be there. It would look suspicious otherwise. I'm telling you, he's come to fetch the wallet.'

Peter looked puzzled. 'So why did he throw it away in the first place?' he said.

Miranda poked her head round the corner. 'Hey!' she said. 'Look at this!'

The Ferret was coming down the ladder, and the wallet was in his hand. Holly, Peter and Miranda watched as he opened the wallet and looked through it. Then he looked through it again, tearing at the lining, turning the wallet inside out. His face grew twitchy with anger. Then he threw the wallet into the gutter, picked up his ladder and walked away.

Holly's breath came out in a *whoosh*. 'He was looking for something,' she said.

'So it can't be the wallet that's important after all,' said Miranda. 'He wouldn't throw it away twice.'

'It must have been something he left in the wallet,' said Peter.

'And the only thing he left in the wallet was the ticket,' said Holly.

'Oh dear, back to that ticket again,' said Peter, shaking his head.

'What's wrong with you?' said Miranda. 'We've got the ticket, haven't we?'

Peter nodded. 'Yes,' he said. 'We've got the ticket, but we still don't know what it's *for*. We're back to square one.'

'Cheer up,' said Holly. 'We've got a mystery on our hands. Even Miranda has to believe that now.'

'I suppose you're right,' said Peter. 'Who knows, we might find out what that ticket is for. All we need is a stroke of luck.'

'Or a stroke of genius,' said Holly.

But it wasn't genius that gave them their precious clue. It was luck – just as Peter had said.

When Holly got home there was a parcel lying on the hall table beside the post and the free newspaper. Holly loved parcels. She liked to guess what was in them before she opened them. She picked it up and felt it. It felt knobbly. What was it?

There was a hard, flat bit, and a softer bit and another smaller bit, which was harder than the other hard bit. And it was hollow.

Shoes. That's what it was. Then she remembered Jamie's shoes. Her mum must have fetched them from the menders.

She was putting the parcel back on the table when she stopped, frozen in mid-action.

It was just an ordinary parcel done up in a brown paper bag. It was just Jamie's shoes. But there was *something* very special about it. There was a ticket with a number on it stuck to the outside.

A blue ticket.

A ticket just like the one they had, except that this ticket had a name printed on it. And underneath somebody had written *Adams* in a spidery scrawl.

Holly pulled the ticket from her pocket and matched it up to the one on the parcel. They were the same colour, the same size – even the perforations matched. The only thing that didn't match was the number.

Holly looked at the printed name at the top of the ticket on the parcel. *Mend-its* it said.

She picked up the parcel and felt it again – just to be sure. Shoes. Was that what their mysterious ticket was for – a pair of shoes the Ferret had taken to the menders? Holly couldn't believe it could be anything quite so ordinary.

She tore back a corner of the paper, just to

be completely sure. It was shoes all right – Jamie's shoes. Her heart sank. Miranda had said it would turn out to be something really ordinary, like a laundry ticket. But *shoes*? How disappointing.

The phone rang. Holly picked it up.

'Hi,' Miranda said breathlessly. 'Have you still got that ticket?'

'Of course,' said Holly. 'But you were right all along. It isn't important.'

'Not important!' Miranda screeched. 'Of course it's important!'

Holly rubbed her ear. Sometimes she wondered why Miranda bothered with the telephone. She only lived three streets away. She could just stand in her back garden and yell.

'Miranda, what are you talking about?' she said.

'Don't move,' she said. 'I'm coming over – and phone Peter. Get him over to your place too. I've got something really amazing to show you!'

Holly was left staring at the phone. What on earth had Miranda discovered?

Miranda and Peter arrived together. Holly

was watching for them. She opened the door just before Miranda reached it. Miranda came rushing through the door, tripped over the doormat and fell flat on her face on the hall carpet.

'Hello, Miranda,' Holly said. 'Nice of you to drop in!'

'Oh, very funny,' said Miranda, picking herself up. 'Why did you open the door like that?'

'To let you in?' Holly suggested.

'You should just have let her crash through,' said Peter. 'She was pounding up the road like a charging rhinoceros. A door or two wouldn't have made any difference to her.'

'If you two go on like that I won't tell you what I've found out,' said Miranda.

Peter grinned. 'I bet you can't help yourself,' he said.

Miranda glared at him. 'It would serve you right if I didn't tell you,' she said, lifting her nose in the air. 'But I'm above that sort of thing.' And she stalked into the sitting-room.

Miranda plonked herself down on the floor and stared up at them.

'Tell us what you've found out,' said Peter.

Miranda looked at him and pursed up her mouth but she couldn't help herself. She was bursting with news.

'Look!' she said. She pulled a newspaper from her pocket and waved it at them.

'What's that?' said Peter.

'This week's free paper,' said Miranda. 'It came today. And look what I found in the small ads!'

She spread the newspaper out on the floor and pointed to an advert halfway down the 'Lost and Found' column.

Reward paid for the return of a light-blue ticket. Lost in the Highgate area.

'What?' yelled Peter, snatching the paper up.

'Let's see,' said Holly. 'Do you think it's the one we found?'

'Of *course* it is,' Peter said. 'Imagine putting an ad in the paper.'

Miranda was nearly popping with excitement. 'It must be really important,' she said.

'So what do we do?' said Peter. 'There's a box number at the bottom of the ad.'

Miranda nodded. 'All we have to do is write to the box number and we'll find the answer to the mystery.'

Holly shook her head. 'You don't have to do that,' she said.

'What?' said Peter.

Miranda looked at her. 'Why not?' she said.

'Because I know what sort of ticket it is,' said Holly.

She went into the hall and brought the parcel in and dumped it down in front of them. 'It's from a shoe-repair shop. That's all. That's our mystery. That man was looking for the ticket to get his shoes back from the menders. He must have left it in his wallet when he threw it away.'

Peter frowned.

'So why would he go to all the trouble of dressing up in overalls to get it back?' he said.

Holly shrugged. 'Maybe Miranda was right,' she said. 'Maybe he really is a bus-shelter mender.'

'But there was nothing wrong with the bus shelter,' Peter said. 'You said so yourself.'

'Why couldn't he just go to the menders and explain he'd lost his ticket?' said Miranda.

'Maybe he did,' said Holly. 'Maybe they wouldn't give him the shoes without the ticket.'

'Like the bus-conductor,' said Peter. 'He wouldn't let us back on the bus without a ticket.'

'So, if he needed the ticket, he had to go looking for it,' said Miranda.

'But dressed as a workman?' asked Holly. 'Peter's right, you know. That really is going over the top.' She thought for a moment. 'I reckon anybody who goes to those lengths must want that ticket very badly.'

'And to do that just to get a pair of shoes back – it sounds fishy to me,' said Peter.

Miranda put her head to one side and narrowed her eyes.

'What are you thinking?' said Holly. 'And don't go all mysterious on us.'

'What if it isn't shoes?' Miranda said.

Holly looked at her. 'What do you mean?' she said.

Miranda frowned. 'Well, you can get other

things done at shoe-repair shops, can't you? Who knows what this ticket is for.'

'What kind of things?' said Holly.

Miranda pursed her lips. 'All the cobbler's shops I know cut keys as well,' she said.

Holly stared at her.

'Miranda, you're brilliant!' she said.

'Don't mention it,' Miranda said.

'So we write to the box number?' Peter asked.

Holly shook her head. 'No, we don't,' she said. 'That guy was far too shifty not to be up to *something*.'

'What *do* we do then?' said Miranda.

Holly looked at them. 'We go and get whatever it was he left at Mend-its,' she said. 'We take that ticket in – tomorrow.'

'And if it's a key?' said Peter.

Holly looked at him, her chin up. 'If it's a key, we'll find out what it opens!' she said.

Bumps in the night

That night Holly started to read her new mystery book, *The Clue of the Broken Angel*.

'Don't read too late,' her mum said when she came in to say goodnight.

'I won't,' said Holly. 'I'm only going to read this chapter.'

'I've heard that before,' said Mrs Adams.

Holly looked at her mum. 'What are you doing with Jamie's Zappa Galactica?' she said.

Mrs Adams ran a hand through her hair. 'Dad has taken it off him,' she said. 'Jamie was driving him mad with it. It makes such a dreadful noise!'

Holly smiled. 'I'm surprised the neighbours haven't complained,' she said.

Mrs Adams laughed. 'At least we'll get a couple of days' peace,' she said. 'Dad says he can have it back the day after tomorrow.

In the meantime he's going to try to find a way to silence it.'

'I don't think Jamie will like that,' Holly said.

'Neither do I,' Mrs Adams said with a shrug. 'Goodnight. And remember what I said about not reading too late.'

But *The Clue of the Broken Angel* was the most exciting mystery Holly had read for ages. She was so involved in it, she even forgot to write down the clues. *Just one more chapter*, she said to herself again and again.

An hour later, the book was finished. Holly closed it and put it on her bedside table. Jamie's space gun was sitting there. Her mum must have put it down and forgotten about it. Holly moved it to one side and looked at her bedside clock.

'Cripes,' she said as she saw the time.

It was nearly midnight. She quickly put out her light and snuggled down in bed. The house was perfectly quiet. Everybody must have gone to bed ages ago.

Holly settled down to sleep, but her mind was full of the book she'd just read. She lay there, going over the plot in her mind. An hour later, she was still wide awake.

There was a sound downstairs. Holly looked at her clock again. Five past one. At this rate she would never be able to get up in the morning. She turned over and closed her eyes tightly.

Sleep! she told herself.

Then she heard the sound again. Like a footstep, on the stairs.

It's your imagination, she told herself. Holly was always thinking she saw suspicious characters – or heard strange noises. And, as her dad often told her, reading mystery books late at night didn't help.

There was a creak. It sounded squeaky. *The fifth stair from the top*, Holly thought. That one and the next one up always creaked. But the next one up had a much deeper creak – more like a groan.

Holly yawned. Then she heard the groaning creak of the next step. Someone was coming upstairs – slowly. Maybe her father had gone downstairs for something. Then she froze. She would have heard if somebody had gone downstairs. There shouldn't *be* anybody downstairs!

Holly's mind began to race. She felt cold despite the warmth of her duvet.

She got out of bed very quietly and crept on bare feet to her bedroom door. Getting down on her knees, she peered round the crack in the door – and gasped.

Someone was coming along the top landing. Suddenly, there was a beam of light, shining on the floor. Not a very strong light. A torch!

Holly put her eye to the crack again. Darkness – except for the torchlight. She looked down. The pool of light from the torch shone on the carpet. As she watched she saw a foot take a step forward. It was a man's foot. All Holly could see was a leg wearing dark trousers and a foot with a rubber-soled shoe. The shoe was funny – half black and half brown leather. Her dad didn't have shoes like that. And anyway he wouldn't be creeping about the house at night with a torch! Holly straightened up. It was a burglar. It really was. She wasn't imagining it this time. And what was she going to do about it?

She stood there, frozen with fear. She had to warn her parents. She bit her lip.

Through the crack she watched the dark shape approaching. Somewhere in the distance she heard the wail of a siren – a police car or an ambulance. It gave her an idea.

Softly she crept over to her bedside table and picked up Jamie's Zappa Galactica. With shaking fingers she found the controls. Then she looked through the crack again. In the street outside, the siren wailed even louder. The man turned to look behind him as the noise got nearer. Holly opened the door another crack and thrust the gun through. Then she pointed it towards the man on the landing. With trembling fingers she pressed the buttons on the control panel.

Immediately the gun started to spout strobes of light. Then it began to whine. The piercing noise rose and the gun began to stutter.

The man spun round. He stumbled, surprised by the lights and turned towards the stairs. Then her parents' bedroom door opened and her father appeared.

'Jamie!' he roared. 'I thought I took that gun away. What on earth are you doing playing with it at this time of night?'

The burglar took the stairs two at a time and Holly shot out of her bedroom.

'It isn't Jamie. It's a burglar,' she yelled at her dad.

Mr Adams rubbed the sleep out of his eyes. 'What?' he said.

Holly pointed to the stairs. Jamie came out of his room. 'My Zappa Galactica!' he said. 'What are *you* doing with it?'

Holly's mother appeared behind her dad. 'What's going on?' she said.

'He's getting away!' Holly cried.

There was a bang as the man wrenched open the front door and let it thud back against the wall. Mr Adams switched on the landing light and Holly dived for the stairs.

The sudden light blinded her for a moment. As she got to the bottom of the stairs she saw the burglar crash through the front gate and turn, running down the road.

'He's gone,' she said turning to the other three who were standing at the top of the stairs.

Mr Adams was looking serious. 'A burglar?' he said.

Mrs Adams came running down the stairs and put her arms round Holly.

'Are you all right?' she said.

Holly nodded shakily. 'I am now,' she said. 'But, Mum, a real burglar is really scary!'

Mrs Adams hugged her tighter.

'A burglar!' Jamie said excitedly. 'Did you scare him away with my gun?'

'I think I'd better ring the police,' Mr Adams said.

'And I'd better make a cup of tea,' said Mrs Adams. 'Come on, Holly, you can come with me. That way I'll know you're safe.'

'What was he like?' Jamie said, running after Holly and Mrs Adams. 'Did he have a mask on?'

While Mr Adams went to the telephone, Holly and Jamie and Mrs Adams went into the kitchen. It was warm and cosy in there and Holly began to stop trembling. Her mum put the kettle on.

'The police are on their way,' Mr Adams said, coming into the kitchen. He sat down at the table and said gently to Holly, 'Perhaps you'd better try to tell us exactly what happened. The police will want to know.'

Holly nodded as her mother handed her a steaming mug of tea. 'I'll try,' she said.

'But I didn't really see him – only his feet.'

By the time Holly had finished telling what she knew the police arrived. There were two of them and they were both very kind.

Holly told them what she had told her parents already but it didn't amount to much.

'We do have a burglar alarm,' said Mr Adams.

The older policeman nodded. 'We had a quick look as we came in,' he said. 'The box was unscrewed and the wire was cut. It looks like a professional job to us – a very professional job.' He looked seriously at Mr Adams. 'You don't keep anything really valuable in the house, do you?' he said.

Mr Adams smiled. 'We don't *have* anything really valuable.'

The policemen looked at each other. 'The best thing to do is to lock up now and get some sleep,' said the younger policeman. 'We'll send someone round in the morning to look for fingerprints but, if you ask me, I don't think we'll find anything. The way that alarm was disconnected points to somebody who knows what they're doing.'

'Fingerprints!' Jamie said. 'Wow! Will you take mine?'

The younger policeman smiled at him. 'If you like,' he said. 'We'll put them on record at Scotland Yard.'

'Wow!' Jamie said again.

But Mr Adams was looking serious. 'It wasn't just somebody trying their luck then?' he said.

The older policeman looked at him. 'It's too early to say yet for sure,' he said. 'But it doesn't look like it.'

Holly heard her mother's voice saying, 'I think it's time you were in bed, Holly.'

She nodded. 'I do feel sleepy,' she said.

The older policeman nodded. 'You've had quite a surprise,' he said, and then he gave Holly a smile. 'In the circumstances, I think you acted very quickly and sensibly, young lady,' he said.

'Oh, Holly's full of good ideas,' Mr Adams said. He smiled, but Holly could see that he was still worried.

'Bed,' Mrs Adams said again. 'You too, Jamie.'

She led them upstairs with Jamie still protesting loudly every step of the way that he wanted to stay.

'Sleep well,' Mrs Adams said as she smoothed Holly's duvet over her.

'Mmmm,' said Holly. But she was almost asleep already. She didn't even hear her mother leave the room.

8 Mend-its

'A *real* burglar?' said Miranda. 'Why didn't you phone me?'

'Oh, sure,' said Holly. 'I just stroll out and say "Excuse me, Mr Burglar, do you mind if I phone my friend Miranda so that she can come round and catch you?"'

'You know what I mean,' said Miranda. 'Oh, I wish I'd been there. If I'd been there we'd have caught him between us!'

'How?' said Holly.

'Trip wires or something,' said Miranda.

Peter laughed. 'Only if you tripped over the wire and landed on him,' he said.

Miranda tried to look down her nose at him but he was too tall. 'And I suppose you'd be full of bright ideas,' she said.

Peter grinned. 'I reckon Holly's idea was pretty good,' he said.

They were on their way to Mend-its on the High Street. Holly had the light-blue ticket in her pocket.

Holly giggled. 'I think I gave him a fright. He practically fell down the stairs.'

'Pity he didn't,' said Peter. 'Then you'd have caught him.'

Miranda sighed. 'It must have been so exciting! What was it like, Holly? You're lucky. Nothing exciting ever happens in our house.'

'It was terrifying,' said Holly.

'So what was he after?' said Peter.

Holly shrugged her shoulders. 'I don't know,' she said. 'We haven't got anything valuable.'

Then she fell silent. Was the burglar looking for . . . the ticket?

No, she thought. *That was silly. Nobody but Peter and Miranda knew I had it*. She shivered. She didn't want to think about anyone else knowing she had it – or what they might do to get it. Somebody might be watching her at this very moment.

'What did the police say?' said Peter.

'I missed them this morning,' Holly said. 'Mum wouldn't let them wake me up. She told them I wouldn't have anything else to tell them and I needed my sleep.'

'What a shame,' Miranda said. 'Did you dial 999?'

'Dad did,' said Holly.

Miranda grinned. 'I've just thought of a joke. What do you get if you dial 666?'

'Don't,' said Peter, getting down on his knees. 'Have mercy. Don't tell us!'

Several people looked in their direction and a woman with a little boy pulled him away from them.

'Get up, idiot,' said Miranda.

'Promise you won't tell us,' he said.

Miranda looked at him, then said, 'An upside-down policeman.'

'Ow!' Peter yelled. 'It hurts!'

Holly dragged him to his feet. 'If you don't stop behaving like a lunatic we'll get arrested,' she said.

Peter got up and looked at Miranda. 'One of these days I'm going to think of the worst joke I know and tell it to you,' he said.

Miranda hooted with laughter and the woman with the little boy looked back at them in alarm.

'That's no good,' said Holly. 'The worse they are, the better she likes them.'

Miranda and Holly laughed.

'So,' said Peter. 'Did the police look for fingerprints?'

Holly nodded. 'But they didn't find any.' She grinned. 'Jamie got them to take his though. He was thrilled!'

Miranda sighed. 'A *real* burglary,' she said. 'A real mystery right under your nose. Too bad you didn't see him.'

'All I saw were his feet,' said Holly. 'He had the weirdest shoes.'

'What do you mean?' said Peter.

'They were black and brown,' said Holly. 'When I told Dad about them he said you call them two-tone shoes.'

'Speaking of shoes,' said Peter. 'There's the shop.' He pointed across the road.

Holly looked. It was a small shop, a typical shoe-repair shop. She cast a glance back over her shoulder and shivered.

'What's wrong?' said Peter.

Holly shrugged. 'I don't know,' she said. 'I've got a feeling somebody is watching us.'

'That's just nerves,' said Miranda. 'No

wonder you're jumpy – after what happened last night. I'd be a complete wreck.' She laughed. 'Hey, what lies at the bottom of the sea and shakes?' she said.

'A nervous wreck,' Holly and Peter said together.

Holly grinned. Peter looked completely beaten but Miranda was making *her* feel better. They crossed the road to Mend-its.

'Here it is,' said Peter. 'Got the ticket?'

Holly produced it from her pocket. 'Here goes,' she said, opening the door and marching in.

An old man looked up from a bench where he was mending a pair of shoes.

'We've come to collect this,' Holly said, handing over the ticket.

The man looked at them over his half-moon spectacles.

'Let me see,' he said, turning away towards a shelf behind the counter. Peter, Holly and Miranda held their breath.

The man turned round, holding a parcel. Peter and Holly looked at each other.

'It isn't a key,' said Miranda.

'What?' said the old man.

Holly gave Miranda a dig in the ribs.

'I said, they aren't for me,' Miranda said. 'They're for her.' She pointed at Holly.

The cobbler handed the parcel to Holly. 'There you go,' he said. He looked at them. 'So he found the ticket, did he?'

Holly looked blankly at him. 'Who?' she said.

'Your dad,' said the cobbler. 'He was in here about half an hour ago. I told him I can't give out things without a ticket. Like the sign says.' He pointed to a handwritten sign on the wall: 'No goods without tickets.'

Holly read the sign. *Please retain your ticket if you wish to reclaim your goods*.

'Quite right,' said Miranda.

The cobbler looked at her. 'Hmm,' he said. 'Well, he made quite a fuss. But I have my reputation to think about. I can't just go giving things out without a ticket.' He looked at Holly. 'And tell your dad he should have taken the shoes back to where he got them. That stitching should never have come out as soon as that.' He peered at the three of them suspiciously. 'In fact, I would have said that the stitching had been cut.'

'Cut?' said Holly.

'That's what it looked like to me,' said the

cobbler. 'But you can't tell – not nowadays. That's what you get these days. Shoddy workmanship. Five pounds twenty please.'

Holly and Miranda and Peter stared at him. That was something none of them had thought of.

Holly looked at the other two as she dug into her pocket.

'I've got two pounds fifty,' she said. 'What about you two?'

The man looked at them even more suspiciously as they counted out the money.

'Didn't your dad give you the money for the repair?'

'He forgot,' Holly said quickly.

'He's got a lot on his mind,' Miranda said helpfully. 'He's a detective.'

The cobbler gave her a narrow look through his spectacles.

'Thanks a lot,' Holly said, taking the parcel and almost shoving Miranda out of the shop.

The cobbler was still looking at them as they left.

'Why did you go and say that?' Holly said as they came out on to the pavement.

85

Miranda shrugged. 'It was the first thing that came into my head,' she said.

'Do you think he suspected anything?' said Peter.

'I don't think so,' said Holly. 'But I reckon we got Miranda out of there just in time.'

Miranda grinned. 'It could have been worse. I could have said he was a lion-tamer or something.'

'I'm surprised you didn't,' Peter said. 'Let's see what's in the parcel.'

'It obviously isn't a key,' said Miranda gloomily.

'It sounded like shoes,' said Holly.

'Maybe it's a bag or something,' Peter said.

Holly looked at the parcel. 'I bet it's just shoes after all.'

'What if it *is* a bag or something and the Ferret undid some stitching to hide secret papers inside it?' said Miranda.

Holly was feeling the parcel, her heart sinking as she did so.

'What's in it?' said Miranda.

'I think you're going to be disappointed,' said Holly.

She opened the brown paper bag and took

out a pair of shoes. They looked quite new, and very ordinary.

'Just a rotten pair of shoes after all,' said Miranda. 'Wouldn't you know it?'

She took the shoes from Holly. 'Look!' she said. 'You can see where they were repaired.' She pointed at the front of the shoes. There was a new line of stitching around each toe.

'Bang goes that theory, then,' said Peter. 'You couldn't hide anything in a pair of shoes.' He turned to Holly. 'We're on the wrong track here,' he said.

But Holly wasn't looking at him. She was looking across the street to where a man was trying to cross the busy road. He was watching them.

'It's him!' she said.

'Who?' said Peter.

'The Ferret!' said Holly.

But just then she saw another man. He was standing in a shop doorway across the road – and his eyes were fixed on the Ferret. As Holly watched, he stepped out of the doorway and began to hurry after the Ferret.

And Holly recognised *him* as well. It was

the man who had been looking at them from the crowd on the day of the parade. The man who had barged into her at the bus shelter when they first found the ticket. And the man she had seen at the Underground station. Holly looked quickly at the Ferret. He was crossing the road now. He didn't seem to know he was being watched. He was making straight for them.

'We'd better give him his shoes,' Miranda was saying.

But Holly's mind was working furiously. Something really strange was going on here.

'Wait a minute,' she said. 'That other guy has been following us.'

'What?' Peter and Miranda said at the same time.

'There's no time to explain,' said Holly. 'Look, the lights are changing!'

The traffic stopped and the Ferret stepped out into the road. The man coming up the other side of the pavement quickened his step.

Holly looked at the second man's feet and breathed in sharply. He was wearing black and brown shoes.

Two-tone shoes.

'It's the burglar!' she said. 'It's him. I'd recognise those feet anywhere!'

Miranda and Peter looked at her open-mouthed.

'We've got to get away,' Holly said urgently. 'Now!' She looked up. The Ferret was across the road now. He looked straight towards her. Holly took a step back. Then she froze. The Ferret's eyes were gazing straight into hers. She couldn't move.

'Come on,' said Peter, grabbing her arm. 'I don't like the look of him.'

Miranda took her other arm. 'Holly!' she said. 'Wake up! We've got to get out of here!'

The Ferret started to run towards them. Behind him, the burglar quickened his pace. But he wasn't looking at them: it was the Ferret he was watching.

Holly dragged her eyes away from the Ferret. She shook her head and blinked.

'Run!' said Miranda.

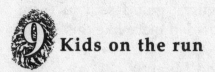 **Kids on the run**

'The shopping centre!' Peter said. 'We could lose him in there.'

Miranda stuffed the shoes back into the paper bag. 'Come on!' she said.

The automatic doors of the shopping centre opened. Peter, Miranda and Holly hurtled through. Peter cannoned into a woman with her hands full of loaded shopping bags. Her bags scattered in all directions.

'Sorry!' Peter said, skidding to a halt.

They wasted a precious minute picking up the bags. A security guard came strolling up and looked at them.

'Kids!' he said to the woman. 'There's nothing broken, is there?'

The woman shook her head. 'I don't think so,' she said.

Holly looked back towards the shopping-centre doors. If the Ferret had seen them come in, he would be right on their trail. She picked up a parcel and stuffed it into one of the bags.

'Walk!' the security guard said to them. 'Running in a crowded place like this is very dangerous.'

Holly, Peter and Miranda backed away – slowly. It was agony. Holly looked down the length of the shopping centre. They *had* to run.

'That guard is still watching us,' said Miranda. 'If the Ferret comes in now, he'll see us.'

'In here!' said Peter. He dragged them into a shop doorway. 'If we can't run, at least we can hide.'

'But he'll see us if he comes in,' Miranda protested.

Peter shook his head. 'We'll see him first.' He pointed to the other side of the doorway. It was mirrored, giving them a great view of the entrance to the shopping centre.

They huddled in the doorway. A shop assistant looked at them suspiciously.

'Try and look as if you're interested in buying something,' Peter said.

'Maybe we should tell the security guard

about the Ferret,' Miranda said. She began to rummage through a basket of videos on special offer in the doorway.

'Tell him what?' said Peter. 'That we stole his shoes?' Miranda's face fell.

Peter turned to Holly. 'How do you know that other guy is the burglar?' he said.

'I recognised his shoes,' Holly said. 'He's been following us.'

'When?' said Miranda. She was clutching a video in her hand.

'At the Underground station yesterday,' Holly said. 'And probably at other times.'

'Why didn't you say?' said Miranda.

Holly looked at her. 'I tried to. But it was bad enough making you believe the Ferret was up to something. Adding another mysterious stranger seemed a bit unlikely – even to me.' She shrugged. 'I thought you'd say it was my imagination.'

'Do you want to buy that?' said a voice. The suspicious shop assistant had come out and was standing looking at the video in Miranda's hand.

'Huh?' said Miranda. Peter nudged her. 'Oh, yes. Sure,' she said.

The assistant took the video from her and

Miranda produced the money. Luckily, she had just enough after paying for the shoes.

Peter looked thoughtful. 'Do you think the burglar was looking for the ticket when he broke into your house? But how did he know you had it?'

Holly looked at the mirror. Still no sign of the Ferret. 'He saw the Ferret throwing the wallet away,' she said. 'I saw him from the top of the bus. He was in the crowd. And I saw him again – when we went back for the wallet the first time. He must have seen us with the ticket. He must have seen me put it in my pocket. And then I saw him again at the Underground station.' She frowned. 'There's some kind of mystery about those shoes.'

'The cobbler said it looked as if the stitching had been cut,' said Miranda.

Peter nodded. 'Maybe the Ferret cut the stitching himself. But why?'

'To hide something inside?' Miranda suggested.

Peter shook his head. 'There isn't any room to hide anything.'

Holly clutched his arm. 'It's obvious,' she said. 'He needed an excuse to take them in

94

to be mended. He had to get rid of them for a couple of days.

'And then he lost the ticket,' said Miranda.

'And we found it,' said Holly.

'And he couldn't get the shoes back without it,' said Peter.

'So what we've got to find out,' said Holly, 'is why anybody would want to get rid of a pair of shoes for a couple of days.' She stopped.

'What is it?' asked Peter. Then his eyes went to the mirror on the other side of the doorway. 'It's the Ferret!' he said.

Indeed, the Ferret was coming in through the doors. As they watched, the burglar also slipped into the shopping centre. His eyes were on the Ferret.

'That's the guy who bumped into you at the bus shelter the other day!' Miranda said to Holly.

Holly nodded. 'I *told* you. He's been following us.'

'I don't like this,' Peter said. 'I think we should go to the police.'

'So do I,' said Miranda. 'But first we have to give those two the slip.'

The Ferret was coming their way. His eyes

were scanning the people in the shopping centre.

'Don't move,' Peter said. 'Maybe he'll walk past. He won't expect us to stay so near the entrance.'

Holly held her breath, her eyes fixed on the reflected image of the Ferret. He was searching the crowd. Then she saw him turn in their direction. His eyes looked straight into hers.

'Oh, no,' said Peter. 'He's seen us in the mirror!'

The Ferret began to quicken his pace.

'Run!' said Peter.

Miranda made for the inside of the shop but Peter dragged her back. 'Not that way,' he said. 'We've got to get away.'

'There's a back entrance to the shopping centre,' said Holly.

'It's beside the escalator and the lifts,' said Miranda.

'Let's go,' said Peter.

'Oi!' said a voice. They turned. It was the shop assistant.

'Don't forget your video,' he said to Miranda.

Miranda grabbed it and dived after Holly and Peter.

Speed was impossible. The shopping centre was crowded. Running and dodging, the three of them wove their way through the crowds.

'He's running too,' Miranda panted, as she glanced quickly over her shoulder.

'It's not far now,' said Holly. 'If we can get out the back entrance, we can lose him in the carpark – can't we?'

Peter's face was looking grim. 'I hope so,' he said.

The shopping centre had never seemed so big or so crowded.

'Round here,' said Holly.

They skidded round the corner by the escalator. The back entrance was there. Holly slowed to a stop. 'Oh, no,' she said.

A notice was pinned to the doors: *Closed for repairs – Please use other entrance.*

Holly's heart sank. Any minute now the Ferret would appear round the corner.

Miranda looked back the way they had come. 'We're trapped,' she said.

'No, we're not,' said Peter. He was looking at the escalators. 'Come on!' He dashed towards the up escalator.

Holly and Miranda followed him as he

jumped on to it.

The escalator was maddeningly slow but they couldn't do anything about it. It was crowded.

They scanned the floor below.

'There he is,' yelled Miranda.

The Ferret was standing looking at the notice on the doors of the back entrance.

Even among large crowds, Miranda's voice was loud.

Below them, the Ferret suddenly turned and looked up – and saw them.

Miranda's face fell. 'Oh, no. I'm sorry,' she wailed.

Holly watched the Ferret. He began to walk towards the escalator.

'He won't be able to push his way up. It's too crowded,' she said. 'We'll still be ahead of him.'

'But what do we do at the top?' said Miranda. 'There's no way out up there.'

'Come on,' Peter was murmuring under his breath. 'Come on, Mr Ferret. Get on the escalator.'

'What?' said Holly.

Peter turned to her. 'If he gets on the up escalator, he'll be stuck. All we have to do is get on the down escalator and we're away.'

Holly watched as the Ferret made his way past the lifts. He was going to get on the escalator. Then his head whipped round as the doors of a lift opened. The Ferret hesitated, then he turned and made for the lift. He got in and the doors closed behind him.

'Oh, no,' said Peter. 'That's all we need. Let's just hope the lift gets stuck.'

'We're nearly at the top,' said Holly. 'We might still make it.'

The upper floor came into view. Holly saw a shoe shop loom up. Outside it, there was a display rail full of shoes. Beyond the shoe shop were the doors to the lift. They were nearly at the top. It wouldn't be long now.

Then she saw the doors of the lift open and the Ferret step out. He stood there in front of the lift, waiting for them.

Slowly the escalator ground its way upwards. There was no chance of escape now. Holly looked at the parcels in Miranda's hands. Then she had an idea.

'Quick!' she said to Miranda. 'Give me the shoes!' Holly made sure she was hidden by the crowd on the escalator, grabbed the paper bag out of Miranda's hands and took the shoes out. Then she gave the bag back to Miranda.

'Put the video in there,' she said.

Miranda looked at her in surprise but she did as she was told.

Holly turned to Peter.

'I've got to get rid of the shoes,' she said. 'Create a diversion. Distract the Ferret's attention. Just give me a couple of moments.'

Peter opened his mouth to ask questions but there wasn't time. The steps of the escalator had flattened out: they were at the top.

Holly watched him anxiously. 'Just *do* it!' she said.

Peter's eyes opened wide, and he began to stagger as the escalator reached the upper floor.

'Aaaaah!' he yelled and he toppled over, bringing Miranda crashing to the ground beside him.

The crowd around them rocked with the impact and somebody pressed the emergency button. The escalator stopped moving.

Holly crouched down and slipped through the crowd. She looked round. The Ferret was pushing his way through the crowd at the top of the escalator. He wasn't looking in her direction. It would only take a moment to hide the shoes. Then she would be back at the top of the escalator.

The security guard was there and a crowd was gathering round. Holly wriggled through. The Ferret was shouting.

'They stole a pair of shoes from me!' he said.

The security guard looked at him. 'Why would they steal a pair of shoes?' he said.

The Ferret gave Peter and Miranda a look. Miranda shrank back, the paper bag in her hands. 'Just get them to hand over that bag,' he said.

The security guard shook his head.

'OK, OK,' he said. 'Keep your hair on.' He turned to Peter and Miranda. 'I might have known you lot would get into trouble. Let's get this sorted out,' he said. 'Let's see what you've got in that bag.'

Miranda looked up and saw Holly. Holly gave her a nod and Miranda handed over the parcel. The Ferret almost snatched it from the security guard. Holly watched his face as he pulled out the video.

'Shoes?' said the security guard.

The Ferret turned on Peter and Miranda. 'Where's the other one?' he said. 'Where's your friend?'

The security guard took a deep breath. 'Now look,' he said, 'I don't know what all this is about but I won't have all this disturbance. There aren't any shoes there.' Then he noticed Holly. 'There's the other one.'

'She's got them!' said the Ferret.

The security guard looked at the Ferret. 'Where?' he said. 'Maybe I'm missing something but the only shoes she's got are the ones on her feet.' He scratched his head. 'Not that I wouldn't like to have a word with this lot,' he said. 'What was all that trouble on the escalator?'

'I tripped,' said Peter.

The security guard shook his head. 'Kids,' he said to the three of them. 'Nothing but trouble. Now you lot just get out of the centre before you cause any more bother.'

He stood there watching them. Holly looked at the Ferret. She could see him wondering where the shoes were.

'Go on,' said the security guard, 'get out of here – the lot of you,' and he looked at the Ferret.

The Ferret turned and began to make his way towards the down escalator. Holly watched him disappear. She felt the back of her neck begin to prickle. She looked round. The burglar with the two-tone shoes was standing a little way off – staring at her. She turned to the security guard. Out of the corner of her eye she saw the burglar melt into the crowd.

'Nutter!' said the security guard as he watched the Ferret disappear. He turned to Peter and Holly and Miranda.

'Right,' he said. 'Out!'

'Aren't you going to arrest him or something?' said Miranda.

'What for?' said the security guard.

'I don't know,' said Miranda. 'Chasing us.'

The security guard shook his head.

'If I had to arrest every oddball that came in here I'd be *very* busy,' he said. 'Anyway, I don't do the arresting. I get in touch with the police on my mobile radio. And don't think you lot can come the innocent with

103

me,' he went on. 'You must have been up to *something*. Off you go now. And don't forget – I'll be watching you.'

Peter and Holly and Miranda watched as he walked away.

'We should have told him,' Miranda said.

'He wouldn't have listened.' said Peter. 'I mean, we *did* steal that guy's shoes, didn't we?'

Miranda looked gloomy. 'I suppose so,' she said.

Peter turned to Holly. 'What did you do with the shoes?' he said.

Holly couldn't help grinning. 'I put them where the Ferret won't find them,' she said.

'Where?' said Miranda.

Holly put her head on one side. 'Guess!' she said.

'Oh, come on,' said Miranda. 'How can we guess?'

'I'll give you a clue,' said Holly. 'Think of that old film I was telling you about: *Charade.*'

Miranda frowned. 'Stamps?' she said. 'Did you post them somewhere?'

Holly laughed and nodded towards the

shoe shop next to the lift.

'Much simpler than that,' she said. 'I put them on the display rail outside the shoe shop.'

'What – just out in the open like that?' said Peter.

Holly laughed. 'It's the best place to hide them,' she said. 'Who's going to notice a pair of shoes among all those other shoes?'

'Just like the film – the stamp on the letter,' Peter said.

Holly nodded. 'And it works!' she said.

'Yeah, until somebody tries to buy them,' said Miranda.

'Oh, no,' said Holly. 'I didn't think of that!'

'We'd better get them,' said Peter. 'Then we can have a good look and find out what's so special about them.'

They turned towards the shoe shop.

'Uh-oh,' said Miranda. She was looking at a tall, thin man standing by the display rail.

'What?' said Holly. Then she saw what was happening. Somebody *was* trying to buy the shoes.

'Just our luck,' Peter said, as the man

picked up the shoes and took them into the shop.

'Come on,' said Miranda. 'We can't let those shoes out of our sight.'

'Try to look casual,' Peter said as they walked into the shop. 'Look as if you're interested in buying shoes.'

'Where is he?' Miranda hissed.

'Over there,' said Holly, trying to look interested in a pair of heavy black boots.

The man was talking to a sales assistant, showing her the shoes.

Holly, Peter and Miranda strolled casually round the display racks nearer to the man and the shop assistant.

'Do you have these in a size ten?' the man was saying.

Miranda groaned as the assistant took the shoes from him.

'I'm afraid these aren't our shoes, sir,' the assistant said. She frowned at them. 'I don't understand what they were doing on our display. Perhaps I should call the manager.'

'Oh, no,' said Holly. 'What do we do now?'

Miranda's eyes lit up. 'Time for some

drastic action,' she said, and darted round the display rack.

'Oh, you've got my dad's shoes by mistake,' she said, taking the shoes smoothly from the assistant. 'He only put them down for a moment to try some others on. Poor man, he's walking about in his socks.' She smiled sweetly and turned away. Her eyes rolled towards Peter and Holly, then towards the door.

Peter and Holly took the hint and the three of them strolled as casually as they could out into the shopping centre.

Holly looked back. The assistant and the customer were looking at them open-mouthed.

'How was that?' said Miranda.

Peter burst out laughing. 'You can collect your Oscar later,' he said. Then his voice died away. He grabbed the shoes out of Miranda's hands.

'Look who it is,' he said, his eyes on the up escalator. 'Our friend, the Ferret.'

Holly swung round. The Ferret was back on their trail.

There was a ping and the lift door opened.

'Come on!' yelled Peter, making a dash for it.

They crowded into the lift and pressed the button. When they got out the Ferret was coming down the escalator, forcing his way through the shoppers.

'I suppose there's nothing else for it,' said Peter. 'Run!'

They ran like mad for the shopping centre entrance. They were running so fast, Holly hardly heard the shouts that followed them. She turned as they pelted through the doors. It was the security guard again. The last thing Holly saw as she hurtled into the street outside was the security guard speaking into his two-way radio.

10 A dead end

'Where are we going?' Holly asked, as they squirmed and pushed their way through the crowds in the High Street.

'To the police,' said Peter over his shoulder. 'I don't know about you, but those guys really scare me.'

Holly glanced over her shoulder. 'Oh, no,' she said.

'What?' panted Miranda.

'The Ferret,' said Holly. 'He's after us again.'

'Quick,' said Miranda. 'Down here!'

She turned into a lane. Holly and Peter pelted after her.

'Where does it go?' said Peter.

'I don't know,' said Miranda, 'but it's better than the High Street. At least we can run.'

'No it isn't,' said Holly. 'It's a dead end!'

There in front of them was a brick wall.

They turned. At the entrance to the lane they could see a figure.

'It's him,' Miranda said, as she shrank back against the wall.

Holly, Peter and Miranda stood there as the Ferret walked down the lane towards them. There was an ugly expression on his face.

They drew closer together.

'There are three of us,' said Holly.

Peter was watching the end of the lane.

'And two of them,' he said.

Holly glanced towards the end of the lane. A man stood there. He was just a dark shape against the light behind him. But Holly still recognised him.

'It's the burglar,' she whispered to Peter.

The Ferret was getting nearer and nearer.

'What are we going to do?' Holly said.

'Give him the shoes,' Miranda said. 'I don't want to get mashed to a pulp just for a pair of shoes.'

Holly took another glance, behind the Ferret. The burglar was walking softly up the lane. Holly frowned. It seemed like he was creeping up on the Ferret.

Then the Ferret said, 'Hand them over.'

'What?' said Peter, trying to pretend he didn't understand.

'The shoes,' he said. 'And be quick about it. I don't have all day.'

'Give them to him,' Miranda said.

But Holly stretched out her hand to stop Peter. 'No,' she said.

Then the other man, the burglar, spoke. 'Oh, no you don't,' he said. 'I'm taking those shoes.'

The Ferret whirled round.

'Quick,' said Holly. 'Run for it!'

She ducked past the Ferret and started to sprint for the opening of the lane. Miranda followed her, but Peter didn't make it. The Ferret turned to him. 'Hand them over,' he growled.

Then they heard the burglar say, 'The law!'

Holly and Miranda turned. There, walking towards them, was a policeman. He was talking into his two-way radio. He looked up as he saw them coming and put his arms out.

'Hey!' he shouted. 'You kids. I want a word with you!'

'There's a man following us,' said Holly.

'Two men,' said Miranda. 'And one of them is a burglar.'

The policeman looked at her. 'Oh, yes,' he said. 'And I've just had a call from the shopping centre about you lot. You've stolen a pair of shoes, haven't you?'

'Not exactly,' said Holly. 'At least, I suppose we have but—'

'No "buts" about it,' said the policeman. 'You kids – you're always up to something. What good are a pair of shoes to you?'

'We don't know,' said Miranda. 'But you've got to listen to us.'

Holly pointed to the Ferret and the burglar. 'It's these two you ought to arrest,' she said. The burglar turned his back, his head down. He pulled up the collar of his jacket.

The policeman looked at Holly. 'I'm just about losing my temper with you lot,' he said. He took out a notebook. 'Now,' he said. 'Names. Let's start with you, sir,' and he looked at the Ferret.

The Ferret licked his lips, then he made a grab for the shoes. Peter took a step back.

'Now, now,' said the policeman. 'No need for that.'

But the Ferret wasn't listening. He made another lunge at Peter. His hands were almost on the shoes.

'Throw them!' Holly shouted to Peter.

Peter raised his hands and threw the shoes. They sailed through the air.

The Ferret jumped and knocked one of the shoes. It bounced off his hand and Holly leaped – and caught it.

The other shoe fell with a thud on the pavement. As it landed, the heel flew off.

The policeman stopped talking. Holly, Peter and Miranda stared at the shoe lying on the pavement. Even the Ferret stopped in his tracks.

There, lying beside the shoe, was a diamond brooch.

'What on earth . . .' the policeman began.

The Ferret began to back away.

'Oh, no you don't,' said the burglar, grabbing him.

The Ferret turned, his face looking very ugly.

'Let me go!' he shouted. 'I don't know what this is about! I don't know anything!'

The burglar made a sound like a snort and the policeman looked at him.

'Well, look who it is,' he said.

The policeman gave the Mystery Kids a look. 'Don't move,' he said. Then he walked towards the two men.

'Well, well,' he said to the burglar. 'If it isn't old Two-Tone. And what have you been up to?'

'He burgled our house last night!' Holly yelled, dragging her eyes away from the diamond brooch.

The policeman looked at her sharply. 'Is your name Adams?' he said.

Holly nodded. Relief flooded through her. At last the policeman was beginning to believe them.

The policeman said a few words into his radio.

The Ferret looked at the burglar. 'See what you've done now?' he said. 'Now we're both for it.'

There was a movement at the end of the lane and two more policemen appeared.

'OK, then,' said the first policeman. 'Let's get down the station and sort this out.' He turned to Peter, Miranda and Holly. 'And

I think you three had better come too,'
he said.

'Amazing,' said the sergeant behind the
desk, scratching his head. 'Imagine you
catching those jewellery thieves.'

Holly, Peter and Miranda smiled. It had
taken them a while to realise that the brooch
was the same one they had read about in the
paper – the one that had been stolen from
the exhibition.

'It was nothing,' Miranda said generous-
ly.

'That's not what Inspector Simmons thinks,'
said the sergeant.

There was a sound in the corridor and the
sergeant stood up straight. 'Here he comes
now,' he said.

Inspector Simmons was a big, gruff man.
He came towards them, smiling.

'Well, well,' he said. 'You kids have
done us a big favour.' He looked round
them. 'Which one of you is Holly Adams?'
he asked.

Holly owned up.

Inspector Simmons gave her an approving
look. 'Your mum and dad told us what you

had seen of your burglar,' he said. 'It was very helpful.'

'But all I saw were his shoes,' said Holly.

The Inspector raised his eyebrows. 'Why do you think he's called Two-Tone?' he said. 'Those shoes are his trademark. As soon as we heard about them we knew who we were after.'

'But how did they do the jewellery robbery?' Miranda said. 'We didn't know anything about that.'

Inspector Simmons shook his head. 'They were quite clever,' he said. 'Two-Tone cut the alarm wires, then the man you call the Ferret sneaked the brooch out of its case, put in a dummy brooch and hid the real one in the heel of his shoe. All he had to do then was walk out of the place, put the shoes in to be mended and, even if he was suspected later, there would be no sign of the brooch.'

'But why was Two-Tone following the Ferret?' said Holly.

'Because the man you call the Ferret decided to trick Two-Tone,' said the Inspector. 'He decided he would sell the brooch and keep the money for himself. But he knew Two-Tone was after him.'

'He saw him – at the parade,' Holly said. 'He threw the wallet away – with the ticket for the shoes in it.'

'And that was his mistake,' said the Inspector. 'Because you saw him throw that wallet away and got suspicious.'

'They don't call us the Mystery Kids for nothing.' Peter said.

Inspector Simmons laughed. 'I've been hearing about that,' he said. His eyes twinkled. 'I'll need to watch out, or you might put us out of a job.'

'Oh, there's no fear of that,' said Holly. 'We were only too glad to see the police.' She turned to the other two. 'Weren't we?' she said.

'Too right,' said Peter.

Inspector Simmons smiled at them. 'I'll need to take some statements from you,' he said. 'I hope you've got good memories.'

Holly dug into her pocket and pulled out the fluffy bunny notebook. 'We've got it all written down in here,' she said. 'All the evidence we collected.'

Inspector Simmons looked at the note-book. 'Hmm,' he said. 'It isn't very official-looking, is it? How would you like a real police notebook?'

Holly, Peter and Miranda looked at one another. Then they grinned.

'*Would* we?' said Peter. He looked at Holly. 'Unless you'd rather stick with the fluffy bunnies.'

Holly grinned. 'Don't knock the bunnies,' she said. 'We did OK with them.'

'But a *real* police notebook,' Miranda sighed.

'A real police notebook would be something else,' said Holly.

Inspector Simmons smiled. 'Wait here,' he said. 'I'll order up three of them. One each.'

'Wow!' said Peter as they emerged from the police station. They were each carrying a brand-new police notebook.

'Now all we need is something to put in them,' said Holly. 'Another mystery.' She bent down and picked up a scrap of paper from the police-station steps.

'What's that?' said Miranda.

Holly peered at it and frowned. 'I don't know,' she said. 'It looks like part of a letter.'

Her eyes lit up. 'Maybe a criminal threw it away when he was being taken into custody. Maybe it's evidence. Maybe we could find the rest.'

'And maybe we've had enough mysteries for one day,' said Peter. He took the piece of paper from Holly, scrunched it up and threw it into a nearby rubbish bin.

'You didn't even try to read it!' Holly said, accusingly.

'I don't care what it was,' said Peter. 'I'm starving. All I want is a burger and a Coke.'

Holly grinned. 'And then we could go back to my place and watch Miranda's video.' She turned to Miranda. 'What did you buy?'

Miranda shook her head as she dug in the brown paper bag. 'I didn't even look,' she said. Then her face broke into a huge grin as she pulled out the video. 'You're not going to believe this,' she said with a shriek of laughter.

'What?' said Peter.

Holly took the video from Miranda and looked at it. Then her face broke into a wide grin as well.

'I don't believe it,' she said to Peter and waved the video at him. 'Look! It's *Charade*!'

119